Illustrations on page 28: © Larousse
Illustrations on page 29: Olivier Raquois
Animal facts: Miguel Larzillière

First edition
2 4 6 8 10 9 7 5 3 1

Library of Congress Cataloging-in-Publication Data
Piquemal, Michel.
[Animalou. English]
Panda / text by Michel Piquemal;
illustrations by Clara Nomdedeu, and Christophe Merlin.
p. cm. – (Abbeville Animals)
Summary: A playful baby panda encounters a leopard. Includes facts about pandas and a game.
ISBN 0-7892-0664-1 (alk, paper)
Pandas—Juvenile fiction.
[1.Pandas—Fiction. 2.Animals—Infancy—Fiction.]
I.Nomdedeu, Clara, ill. II.Merlin, C. (Christophe), ill. III. Title. IV. Series.

PZ10.3.P416 Pan 2000
[E]—dc21   00—026186

Abbeville Animals

Panda

By Michel Piquemal

Illustrations by Clara Nomdedeu and Christophe Merlin

Translation by Roger Pasquier

Abbeville Kids

A Division of Abbeville Publishing Group

New York • London • Paris

How naughty Bei Bou is! Instead of eating bamboo, he is playing, climbing, and jumping from one bamboo stalk to another. . . .

"Eat!" says his mother.

Bei Bou nibbles a piece, then scrambles up a big bamboo.

His mother calls, "Get down from there, Bei Bou!"

He jumps, and lands on all fours.

It's time for a nap. Bei Bou
closes one eye, but as soon as his
mother falls asleep, he gets up.
He wants to keep playing, so he
goes off in search of adventure.

Bei Bou comes to a clearing.
He hears a strange noise.
Curious, he goes closer.

Pandas don't build themselves a nest or den. They sleep on the ground or on a tree branch.

Pandas must eat bamboo all day long to survive. When they are not eating, they sleep.

Adult pandas have no enemies. But babies may be eaten by leopards, jackals, wolves, and some large birds of prey.

A leopard is hiding beneath some large leaves. He jumps out, shows his teeth, and growls. "Grrr . . . I'd gladly gobble a baby panda for breakfast."

Bei Bou turns and scurries away. He runs and runs.

But the leopard is faster. . . .

"Mother! Mother! Save me!" cries Bei Bou, out of breath.

Bei Bou's mother suddenly appears out of a thicket. She stands on her hind legs and shows her claws.

Surprised, the leopard steps back.

Pandas normally walk with all four feet flat on the ground.

Pandas can stand on their hind legs to climb trees, or to scare animals that are threatening them.

But the leopard isn't frightened. He growls even louder and shows his teeth. Bei Bou, shaking all over, hides behind his mother. The leopard looks ferocious. Will he pounce? Bei Bou doesn't want the leopard to fight with his mother. What can he do?

Pandas climb well, thanks
to their claws.

Pandas do not live in families. The
male lives alone, while the female
takes care of her young until it is
two or three years old.

Bei Bou climbs a tree. Seeing his lunch vanish, the leopard turns away. He can't catch the baby panda. Bei Bou is too high, right at the top of a tall birch tree. Sitting on a branch, he makes faces at the leopard. He calls out, "Can't catch *me*!"

Pandas have six "fingers," and can grip things in their front paws.

Pandas live in bamboo forests, with a few birch and maple trees.

"Don't be so sure," snarls the leopard. He climbs after Bei Bou, reaches his branch, and crawls closer and closer. . . .

But then the branch cracks. *Crash!* The leopard tumbles down, and Bei Bou jumps safely to the next tree.

"Ow! Ow! Ow!" moans the leopard as it limps away.

Pandas are very acrobatic, and know how to take long, dangerous jumps.

19

A mother panda sometimes gives birth twins, but she only has enough milk for one to survive. Mother pandas are gentle affectionate and take good care of their you

Bei Bou scrambles down from the tree. "Hooray, mother, we won! Did you see how I climbed? And I wasn't even afraid!"

His mother starts to scold him, but Bei Bou jumps into her arms. And then all she can do is give him a hug.

All About Pandas

The panda lives in China in the mountains where forests of bamboo grow. Pandas are shy and difficult to observe.

The panda must eat enormous quantities of bamboo, which is almost its only food. It spends up to sixteen hours a day eating between thirty and ninety pounds of bamboo.

To eat, pandas sit on the ground and bring food to their mouths with their front paws.

The male and female are very similar. The female is just a little smaller and has lighter black patches.

At birth, a baby panda is blind, and weighs only three ounces. A baby panda spends the first four months of its life in its mother's arms.

Over the years, people have destroyed much of the bamboo forests where pandas need to live. Today, it is one of the rarest animals in the world. Only one thousand survive in the wild.

The panda has become an international symbol for the protection of wildlife. The Chinese government has declared it a "national treasure" and it is the logo of the World Wildlife Fund. By replanting bamboo forests, they hope to save the panda.

On all fours, the panda is between three and five feet long. It can stand over five feet tall, the height of an adult person.

The panda's black and white fur is dense and waterproof. The fur protects the panda from cold and snow.

Under its tail, the panda has a gland that makes a distinct scent. To let other pandas know of its presence, the animal rubs this gland against tree trunks.

Each foot has six "fingers," and the front feet can hold things like bamboo.

The panda weighs between 150 and 325 pounds, the weight of one or two adult people.

With its round head, the panda looks like a teddy bear. It never moves its ears or shows its teeth.

The black fur surrounding its eyes makes them difficult to see. The pupils narrow to slits like those of a cat do.

The jaws are very powerful. They have to crush hard bamboo stalks.

Follow the Path

Have fun following the panda's path and answering the questions

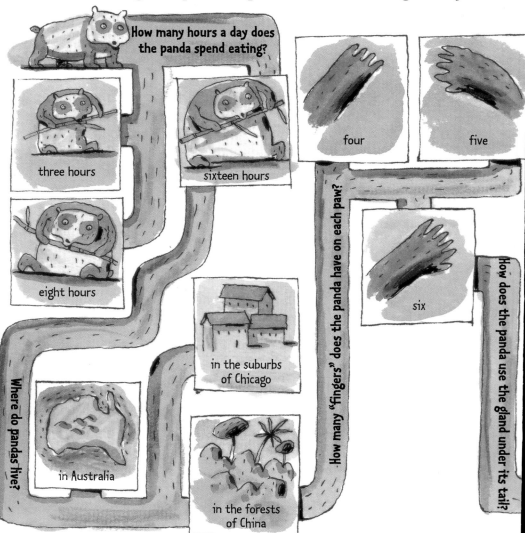

How many hours a day does the panda spend eating?

three hours

sixteen hours

eight hours

four

five

six

How many "fingers" does the panda have on each paw?

How does the panda use the gland under its tail?

Where do pandas live?

in the suburbs of Chicago

in Australia

in the forests of China

he has longer ears

he is larger

Which is an enemy of the baby panda?

How do you tell the male from the female?

he sings badly

the elephant

the leopard

the mouse

to mark trees with its scent

to pee

Relatives

For a long time, scientists thought pandas were related to raccoons. Now they have found pandas are actually related to bears. But bears and raccoons had a common ancestor millions of years ago.

The polar bear is the largest of bears. It lives in the Arctic and feeds on fish and seals. It has no fear of people, and can be very dangerous.

The brown bear is almost as large and heavy as the polar bear. It hibernates through the winter, and wakes up, much thinner, in spring.

The lesser panda, although it eats lots of bamboo, is definitely a member of the raccoon family. Because of its beautiful rusty fur, it is called the red panda or "fire fox."

The honey badger adores honey. Its flexible lips form a straw when it sucks up ants and termites.

The raccoon, smart and adaptable, uses its paws like hands. It lives in North American forests, but may come to houses in search of food.

The coati lives in tropical forests of North and South America. Very agile, it spends most of its time in trees, which it descends head first. It uses its long snout to search for food—fruit, insects, spiders, and lizards.